MARC BROWN

KU-586-758

ARTHUR
and the Baby

LITTLE, BROWN AND COMPANY
New York   Boston

**MORAY COUNCIL
LIBRARIES &
INFO.SERVICES**

20 32 51 71

Askews & Holts

JA

◇ FOR TOLON, TUCKER AND ELIZA ◇
my three babies

Copyright © 1987 by Marc Brown

All rights reserved. Except as permitted under the U.S. Copyright Act of 1976, no part of this publication may be reproduced, distributed, or transmitted in any form or by any means, or stored in a database or retrieval system, without the prior written permission of the publisher.

Little, Brown and Company
Hachette Book Group
237 Park Avenue, New York, NY 10017
Visit our website at www.lb-kids.com

Little, Brown and Company is a division of Hachette Book Group, Inc.
The Little, Brown name and logo are trademarks of Hachette Book Group, Inc.

The publisher is not responsible for websites (or their content) that are not owned by the publisher.

First Edition: June 2011
Originally published under the title *Arthur's Baby*

Arthur® is a registered trademark of Marc Brown.

Library of Congress Cataloging-in-Publication Data

Brown, Marc Tolon.
[Arthur's baby]
Arthur and the baby / by Marc Brown. — 1st ed.
p. cm.
Previously published in 1987 under title: Arthur's baby.
Summary: Arthur isn't sure he is happy about the new baby in the family, but when his sister asks for his help in handling the baby, Arthur feels much better.
ISBN 978-0-316-12905-3
[1. Babies—Fiction. 2. Brothers and sisters—Fiction. 3. Aardvark—Fiction.] I. Title.
PZ7.B81618Agr 2011
[E]—dc22
2010038298

10 9 8 7 6 5 4 3 2 1

SC

Printed in China

"We have a surprise for you," said Mother and Father.
"Is it a bicycle?" asked Arthur.

"We're going to have a baby!" said Mother.

"Ooooo," squealed D.W. "I love babies!"

"A *baby*?" said Arthur.

"Yes, in about six months," said Father.
"Plenty of time for us all to get ready."

Arthur's friends had lots of advice.
"Better get some earplugs," said Binky Barnes,
"or you'll never sleep."

"Forget about playing after school," said Buster.
"You'll have to babysit."

"You'll have to change all those dirty diapers!"
said Muffy.

"And you'll probably start talking baby talk,"
said Francine. "Doo doo ga ga boo boo."

For the next few months, everywhere
Arthur looked there were babies — more
and more babies.
"I think babies are taking over the world!"
said Arthur.

"Don't look now," said Buster,
"but you could be in for triple trouble."

One day after school, D.W. grabbed
Arthur's arm.
"I will teach you how to diaper a baby," she said.
"Don't worry about diapers," said Mother.
"Come sit next to me. I want to show you
something."

Arthur age 9 months

"Is that really me?" asked Arthur.
"Yes," said Mother. "You were such a cute baby."

Arthur age 1 year

D.W. age 2 months

"Look," said D.W. "This is me with Mommy and Daddy. Don't I look adorable?"

D.W. age 5 months

That Saturday morning, Mother took out her suitcase.

"Where are you going?" asked Arthur.

"The baby could come any day now," said Mother.

"I need to be ready for the hospital."

"Here," said D.W. "Something for you to look at while you're there."

Sunday morning, Arthur and D.W. found
Grandma Thora fixing breakfast.
"You have a new sister!" she said.
"Yippee! Yippee! Yippee!" said D.W. "She'll be
just like me!"
"That's what I'm afraid of," said Arthur.

The next day, they went to the hospital to see the new baby.

"We named her Kate," said Father.

"I think she has your nose, Arthur."

"I think she has D.W.'s mouth," said Arthur.

On Tuesday, Mother and Father brought Kate home.
Everyone was acting like they'd never seen
a baby before.
Every time the doorbell rang, more presents arrived.
"They're not for you, Arthur," said D.W.
"They're for the baby."

"Arthur, don't you want to try holding Kate?"
Mother asked.
"Can I have another turn first?" asked D.W.
"It's Arthur's turn," Mother said.
"I'd rather look," said Arthur.
"It's just as well," said D.W.
"Arthur doesn't know beans
about babies."

A few days later, Mother needed some help.
"I have to go upstairs," she said. "Arthur, would
you watch Kate?"
"*Me*?" asked Arthur. "What do I do?"
"Don't worry," said D.W. "I'll take care
of everything."

When the doorbell rang, D.W. answered the door. "Arthur can't play," she said. "He has to babysit. But you can come in and see my baby."

"Don't get too close, because you all have germs!
And be quiet," D.W. said, "my baby is sleeping."

"Look!" said Francine. "She opened her eyes."
"Stand back," said D.W. "She wants her bottle."

Kate drank her bottle in a flash.

Then she began to cry.
"Everyone remain calm," said D.W.

D.W. gave Kate a kiss.
Kate cried louder.

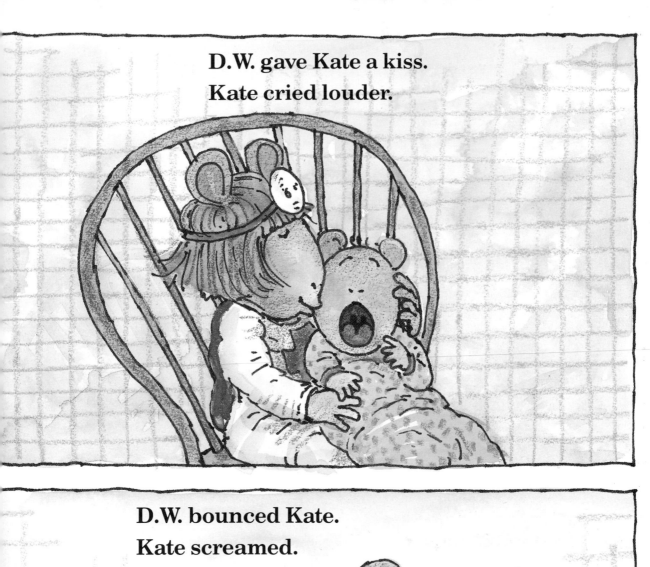

D.W. bounced Kate.
Kate screamed.

"Arthur, quick! Do something!" D.W. said.
"She's your baby, too."
"All of a sudden she's *my* baby," said Arthur.
"Why is she crying?" asked D.W.
"She's trying to tell you something," said Arthur.
"What?" asked D.W.
"Listen carefully," said Arthur.

"Burp!" said Kate.
"Is everything all right?" asked Mother.
"It is now," Arthur answered.